"KAYLA AND JOY HAVE CREATED A WORLD WHERE CHILDREN CAN IMAGINE THEMSELVES, COMPLETE WITH POSITIVE ROLE MODELS AND FUN FILLED ADVENTURE."

~Kevin Meagher~
Television Producer
Owner, Production Company

"ORIGINAL, UNIQUE, TIMELY."

~Marilyn Sachs~
Award Winning Author of
Veronica Ganz & The Bears' House

"TOE-TAPPIN' FUN WITH AN URGENT, POSITIVE MESSAGE FOR OUR YOUNG PEOPLE."

~George Peter Tingley~
Composer of "Kristi's Theme"
for Gold Medalist Kristi Yamaguchi
Composer for Alfred Publications

"AN AWESOME READ. THE COMBINATION OF STORYTELLING WITH A GREAT MESSAGE IS PERFECT FOR EVERYONE.
GO EARTH-GUARDS! GO GREEN!"

~Randy Phillippe~
LetsGoGreenKids.com
Songwriter and Co-creator

Case of The Poisoned Lake

First edition published by

Pockets Productions and Publishing
P.O. Box 386 Novato, Ca. 94948
415-305-8485
earth-guards@earth-guards.com
www.Earth-Guards.com

Library of Congress Control Number: 2010936085

ISBN (13) 9780982965900

The Case of the Poisoned Lake
Earth-Guards Adventure Team

Created by Joy Evans
Written by Kayla Gold
Illustrations by Catie Vercammon-Grandjean
Book layout and art direction by Joy Evans
Theme song lyrics and music by Kayla Gold

Published in the United States of America
Printed by Tien Wah Press in Singapore

Case of The Poisoned Lake

EARTH-GUARDS™
ADVENTURE
TEAM

CREATED BY
Joy Evans

WRITTEN BY
Kayla Gold

ILLUSTRATED BY
Catie Vercammen-Grandjean

THIS BOOK IS DEDICATED to everyone who believes in the power of creative vision and the brilliant potential of the human mind.

ACKNOWLEDGEMENTS: We want to thank all the young readers who provided excellent editorial feedback: Adam, Rebecca, Mackenzie, Lucas, Delaney, Emilie, Chloe, Sarah, Eric, Jane, Caroline, Sawyer, Natalie, Jack, and Ananya.

OUR SPECIAL THANKS TO Derek Wilson, Michael Whiteley, Cindi Valverde, Elizabeth Dunlavy, and Kevin Meagher for giving us their unselfish time. To Mom and Dad (Dan & Tanette Goldberg), and to our friends and family for their wonderful comments, generous support and for believing in our project.

THE MISSION of *Pockets Productions and Publishing* is to INSPIRE young minds to think outside the box and find new solutions to environmental challenges around the world.

Case of The Poisoned Lake

An Earth-Guards Adventure

Table of Contents

Table of Contents Continued

The Earth-Guard Pledge

As a member of
The Earth-Guards,
I pledge to
respect and be a
steward of the Earth
so that it has
clean water, fresh air,
rich soil, and healthy forests
for all
future generations.

Prologue

LEAF, POTO, NIMBLE, POCKETS, AND ZOHNA met while playing on the mountain near their homes. Except for Leaf, all of them were newcomers to the Town-Below-The-Mountain. Their families had been forced from their original homes by man-made mishaps or poisonous disasters. They wished they could do something to foil any foul play that could cause such environmental upheaval. But, they were just kids.

THERE WAS also the horse, Mercury. Zohna had rescued him from certain death...but that's another story.

ONE DAY, they found a strange passageway inside an old log.   But, this wasn't any old log. This was Old Man Log and it was magical.

THE PASSAGEWAY led to a cave where great twisted roots plunged and merged into all sorts of patterns. One huge, thick root came straight down from the top of the cave and pulsed with a strange light. It gave each of them special superpowers.

NOW they were more than five friends—and one horse. Now, they COULD do something. They became "The Earth-Guards Adventure Team".

THEIR MISSION: To right all toxic wrongs...one dirty guy at a time.

Meet The Earth-Guards

Leaf

Valiant Leader
and
Clairvoyant Pathfinder

Poto

Sparkling Gem
and
Passionate Daydreamer

Nimble

Stouthearted Powerhouse
and
Engineering Dynamo

Trusted Troubleshooter
and
Quantum Pioneer

Zohna

Vivacious Truthseeker
and
Self-Reliant Trailblazer

Constant Companion
and
Bravehearted Ally

Beware The Dirty Guys

Onebrow Care-not

Publicly Incompatible
and
Environmentally Insane

Toxic Tinkerer
and
Frozen-cistic Diva

FLYING UPHILL

CHAPTER 1

An Earth-Guard Adventure

LEAF STEPPED ON THE Bramble Mat and gave the command, "We fly". The Mat rose a few feet off the ground and started up the mountain path. It tilted to one side. Leaf quickly shifted his balance and straightened it out. "Nice work," he said to himself. After another 20 feet, it tilted more sharply. One side dipped down with a jerk while the other side spiked violently into the air. It was like a dinner plate when you accidentally put your elbow on the edge and your entire meal spills "splat" onto the floor. Leaf was not able to get his balance this time and he tumbled off the Bramble Mat like a spoonful of mashed potatoes. "Urg," he said as he got a mouthful of dirt. That kind of thing was not supposed to happen now that he had superpowers.

Leaf was trying to fly his Bramble Mat uphill. That's right, a Bramble Mat. It was a sticky, prickly rug made out of roots, thorns, and branches. Leaf was the only who had the power to touch it without getting pricked. And, it could fly. Leaf could stand on it like a skateboard and surf the breezes along the flat paths at the bottom of the mountain. He could sail

1

it downhill, too. No problem. Learning to fly uphill, however, was harder. A lot harder.

His life had changed so much since the beginning of summer, only a few months ago. Then, he was a normal 11-year-old boy who played the saxophone and rode a skateboard. Now, everything was different. He had superpowers and was learning to fly on a Bramble Mat.

Actually, "different" was an understatement.

TWO MONTHS EARLIER

CHAPTER 2

An Earth-Guard Adventure

IT WAS THE BEGINNING of summer. As the final bell rang at school, Leaf headed for the mountain.

"Leaf," he heard a voice call from behind him. "Wait up." It was Poto. She was a girly girl but he liked her anyway. "Where are you going?" she asked and then without waiting for an answer added, "Can I come?"

"I thought you had summer swim team," he answered.

"That doesn't start until next week. I went up a level." Poto had moved to the Town-Below-the-Mountain last year. Her family was from an island and she used to spend a lot time playing in the waves.

"I bet you can swim faster than almost everybody."

"Almost," Poto laughed.

"You must miss the ocean."

"Yeah... a lot,"

"The reason you had to move...is it really true?" Leaf said.

Poto looked down and sighed, "Yeah. The coral reef was dying and the fish started to disappear.   There weren't enough fish to catch. My parents have friends here who offered them new jobs."

"You want to go back there, don't you?" Leaf asked.

"Well...yeah, if there are ever any fish again."

Leaf and Poto walked a little farther not saying anything. Poto finally broke the silence, "I told Pockets about Old Man Log.   Can we show it to him?"

Pockets was a new boy in town and smarter than the science teacher.   He wore cargo pants with lots of pockets so he could carry around the crazy gadgets he invented.

Leaf answered, "Sure."

"I'll go get him," Poto said.   "He's probably in the science lab as usual."

Leaf shook his head, "No, I think he left there. He's in the computer room."

"How do you know?"

Leaf hesitated before answering, then said quietly, "Sometimes, I...I...just get a feeling about things."

Poto looked at him quizzically, then nodded, "Okay. We'll meet you at the log."

4

OLD MAN LOG

CHAPTER 3

An Earth-Guard Adventure

LEAF WAS THE ONE WHO had named Old Man Log. Leaf had named everything on the mountain. He was born in the Town-Below-The-Mountain, and from the time he could walk, he hiked the trails with his dad. His real name was Tom, but his father had been the local expert on trees so he ended up with the nickname Leaf, and it stuck. When Leaf was 7, his dad died in a freak accident while working on a project in the Misty Forest. Leaf remembered that day well. He had woken up with a bad feeling.

Since then, Leaf spent most of his time on the mountain because it always made him feel better. He explored its gulches, streams, hillsides and trails. There was the gully at the top of the first peak that snaked its way westward. Leaf named it "Rattlesnake Ravine". The "Far-and-Yonder Road" was the name Leaf gave the fire road that wound up from the base of the mountain. It went to the highest ridge and continued into the distance farther than he could see.

Then, there was the huge tree trunk that had

fallen inside a stand of oak trees. It was dead and rotting. Dry wood swirled around a big eyeball-shaped knothole. Next to it, the splintered end of a broken, long-forgotten branch stuck its nose out proudly. No matter what angle you saw it from, this dead tree appeared to have a face, a gentle old man's face like the face of your grandfather's grandfather...the one on the nice side of the family. Leaf named it "Old Man Log". When no one was looking, he would talk to it.

"Hey, Old Man," he would joke, "lying down on the job, eh?" Leaf would pause and pretend to hear an answer, then continue. "I saw six lizards at Lizard's Lair today. Six. But, no Bobcats at the Crossing." Then, he would give the log a good-natured slap and say, "Okay, see ya around."

On that first day of summer, Leaf wanted to talk to Old Man Log before Pockets and Poto showed up. He walked up the big hill that led from town. It leveled out at Cricket Thicket, which was the trailhead for several mountain paths. From there, he followed Skinned Knee Path to the clearing in the stand of oak trees.

"Hey Old Man, ready for summer?" he said. "It's gonna be a scorcher."

He sat down, picked up a stick that lay nearby and poked the wood. It was soft and gushy, and had deteriorated more since his last visit.

6

He ripped off a splinter where the wood was breaking. A little gap appeared. As Leaf pulled on one side of the gap, it opened wider, like the log was yawning. How strange. Looking in, Leaf blinked twice, and looked again. Yes, this is very strange. There was a passageway inside the log that disappeared into the ground. Leaf stepped into the log, dropped beneath the dirt and crawled a few feet on his hands and knees. The passageway grew bigger, and if he bent his head a little, he could stand up and walk through it.

It led to a cave where twisted roots plunged and merged into all sorts of patterns. Huge gnarled roots draped from the ceiling and pierced the floor. Smaller roots forked out on all sides of the bigger ones and curved around to connect with each other. Leaf began exploring this jungle-like maze, climbing all over the intricate woody web. What a cool place. It was going to be an amazing summer.

"Leaf, " voices called from the passageway. "Are you in there?" It was Poto and Pockets.

"You gotta see this!" he called back.

In a few minutes, they stepped into the cave.

"Oh my," Poto said looking around. She ran her hand over a few of the shapes made by the crisscrossing roots. "It's beautiful."

"Shhh," said Pockets. "Someone else is here." Sure enough, there were voices coming from across the cave. They all froze, held their breath and listened.

SILHOUETTES

CHAPTER 4

An Earth-Guard Adventure

VOICES AND THE CLIP-CLOP of horse's hooves echoed in the cave as a tall portal opened up directly across from where Leaf, Pockets and Poto were standing. Slanted sunlight slid in like a letter under a door and cast a hazy light across the curlicue root patterns. Three silhouettes appeared against the backdrop of the outside light.

"Look at this crazy place," one of them said.

"Can this be for real?" the other replied.

Leaf recognized one of the voices. "Nimble?" he asked.

"Leaf?" Nimble answered, "What are you doing here?"

Nimble was a 15 year-old from the high school engineering team and the only older kid from town who was nice to Leaf. As Nimble walked further into the cave, Leaf could make out his features in the dimness. The two other silhouettes were Zohna and her horse Mercury. Imagine that—a horse walking into a cave. Zohna was a year younger than Nimble, and a down-to-earth, no-nonsense girl with a beautiful, piercing gaze. Nimble and Zohna had both

moved to the Town-Below-The-Mountain last December.

"How'd you get in here?" Leaf asked them.

"I was helping Zohna look for some plants for her science project."

"Stinging nettles," Zohna replied. "It's a natural medicine. Cures all kinds of things."

"We were near Hidden Lake when we saw a big opening under an outcropping of rock."

"Big enough for Mercury," said Zohna.

"I swear it wasn't there before," Nimble said.

Suddenly, the large root in the center of the cave began to pulse with a yellow light, like the heartbeat of a huge glowworm. Leaf felt drawn to the rhythm of the eerie glow and moved closer.

"No, Leaf, don't," Poto warned.

The others spoke all at once, "Careful." "No." "What is that?" "What's going on?" "Leaf, watch out."

CHOSEN

CHAPTER 5

An Earth-Guard Adventure

LEAF DID NOT LISTEN to the warnings from the others. He walked straight to the root, hand outstretched and grabbed hold. It was like plugging into a giant wall socket and he lit up like a firefly. Leaf, the human firefly. The light ballooned out and flooded the entire cave. A voice spoke. It was robust, deep and musical like the lowest notes on Leaf's saxophone.

"Ahh! You have arrived," it said. "You are all here."

"Woah, dude" Nimble whispered.

Mercury got spooked and jerked back on the reins, "Easy boy," Zohna calmed him.

The voice continued, "I am the living root of the once great tree you call Old Man Log. There is magic in this mountain…"

Leaf always had a feeling this mountain was special.

"….and it has brought all of you here."

Leaf glanced at the others, then looked back at the root, "Wha…what for?"

"…to right all toxic wrongs."

"Oh right," Nimble was sarcastic. "Like we can do that."

"There are many who will help you. But there are some whose trashy thinking makes them dangerous. These are known as the Dirty Guys. You must work to change their grungy ways."

"How?" asked Zohna.

"This is too weird," said Nimble.

The voice deepened, "You will be given super-powers based on talents you already possess. Use those powers for good and they will continue to grow."

"Superpowers, wow," said Pockets.

"Why us?" Leaf asked.

"You have all suffered from the effects of Humankind's disconnection with the breath of Earth..."

Leaf knew that was true for him and Poto. Now he wondered about Pockets, Nimble and Zohna, too.

"...but you have retained your pure hearts. And, just as important, you have the desire."

"He's right," Poto said. "I wish I could bring the fish back to my island."

The voice continued, "Leaf, you have an unique ability to see the unseen. You will lead."

"I will?" Being the youngest, Leaf was not sure that Old Man Log was choosing correctly.

"Your missions will present themselves to you in due time. Until then, do your best. All of you...always do your best."

14

The light faded. Leaf stood still and stared at the root.

"What just happened?" Poto asked.

Pockets replied, "I think our lives are going to be very different from now on."

SUPERPOWERS

CHAPTER 6

An Earth-Guard Adventure

LEAF WENT BACK TO THE CAVE several times that summer, though the root of Old Man Log only spoke with him twice.

The first time, it directed him to look beneath a particularly twisted-up patch of roots, "You will ride the wind." Leaf felt the blood rush through his entire body when he pulled the Bramble Mat from under the dirt. Dark twigs on the front spelled out the words, "We Fly."

The second time the root spoke, it described the dirty guys that were likely to be nearby. That unnerved Leaf for the rest of the day.

Leaf's first task as leader was to come up with a name. "Toxic Avengers"? Good, but someone had already thought of that. "Stewards of the Earth"? Nah, too long. "The Dirt Defenders"? Close, but not quite. "Earth-Guards". Yes, that sounded impressive, and when he presented it to the others, they liked it, too.

Everyone's superpowers began to develop that summer. Leaf thought his powers where growing far too slowly. In June, he could play super-fast riffs on his saxophone, but it wasn't until the beginning of August, that he got all the notes right. In early July, he had learned to fly his Bramble Mat in small hops, but it took three more weeks before he could stay off the ground for more than 20 feet. He still could not fly uphill.

Toward the end of summer, Leaf noticed a new ability. When he sat very still, he could hear and see things clearly that were far away. The visions occurred randomly, popping into his head out of control.

It was early September and school had just started. The first week was annoying since it was Indian summer and still hot outside. No one wanted to be inside in this weather.

Friday afternoon finally arrived which meant everyone would come to the mountain. Each Earth-Guard had called dibs on a specific location as their personal home base. Leaf had chosen a massive oak tree a half-mile up the Far-and-Yonder-Road. It was so huge it took 50 giant steps to walk around the area shaded by its branches. There was always a breeze here that made the leaves shimmy, so Leaf named the tree Dancing Oak. From here he could see Cricket Thicket and most of the south side of the mountain. It was also a good place to catch the wind for flying practice, though he had his fill of practice for today. He sat down with his back against Dancing Oak's great trunk.

At that moment, there was a rumbling in the

distance. It surged closer and louder, like an ocean wave rushing toward shore. The ground began to vibrate. Within seconds, Zohna on her horse Mercury came galloping wildly up the trail, a cloud of dust rising in their wake. As they sped by, Zohna called out, "We're racing Nimble to the other side. See ya later." Her voice trailed off and Mercury's hoof beats faded as quickly as they had begun. A minute later, Nimble whooshed by on his flybercycle, a radical looking motorcycle he had built from the ground up. It was quiet, clean...and fast. He flashed a smile at Leaf and kept going.

"Well, Zohna and Nimble are here," Leaf-thought, "and Mercury's winning. He's gotten faster."

Poto and Pockets would be coming up the hill from town anytime now. Leaf played a few quiet notes on his saxophone to pass the time, as he kept watch. Ah, there they are. Poto and Pockets waved good-bye to each other and took separate trails. Pockets turned right; Poto turned left toward her pond at the base of Ribbit Creek.

Since Leaf had not seen Poto all day at school, he thought he would go bug her for fun. He slung his saxophone over his shoulder, stepped onto the Bramble Mat and flew down the mountain.

Leaf at Poto's Pond

CHAPTER 7

An Earth-Guard Adventure

WHERE DID SHE GO? Leaf watched as Poto quickly disappeared beneath the opal colored water. A minute ago, her magic cape had grown longer, wrapped around her legs and morphed into a sparkling blue-green tail. The rest of it fused with her body to form a second skin of shimmering teal. Her eyelids became clear. The change was complete. Poto had become a mermaid. With a curving leap, she plunged deeply into the water.

Poto was the only one who could transform like that. Every time Leaf saw it happen, he felt like he was in a fantasy movie. Hard to believe it was real. Leaf looked out over the water, expecting to see Poto gracefully swimming and twirling. Instead, she was bobbing on the surface, one shoulder down, haphazardly splashing with her other arm.

"Stupid air bubble," she complained.

Transforming into a mermaid was still new for her and it did not always go well. An air bubble was caught on her right side underneath her sleek scales. As soon as she had dived in, it had buoyed her back up like a bouncing ball. She was stuck on her side thrashing about awkwardly trying to smooth the bubble away.

She ran her hands over the bubble, but it slipped to the back of her tail throwing her face first into the water. She arched back to reach for it with both hands, but it zipped around to the front tossing her on her back. It was like chasing a cricket or a lizard. You almost get it and then it skitters away. She looked ridiculous flailing about like that and Leaf announced playfully, "Poto versus the Mighty Air-bubble. Tonight on cable."

Poto scowled at him, "Just you wait." With one more resolute motion, she sent the bubble to the base of her fins where it finally escaped with a little "puff".

"What a relief," she said and dove into the pond slapping her tail triumphantly on the surface. No sooner had she disappeared, than she burst back up, curved in the air, arched perfectly, and splashed down hard drenching Leaf.

"Gotcha!" Poto laughed.

"Hey, watch out or I'm going to play my saxophone right in your face!"

"Cooool," she said diving into the water again, scales glinting in the sunlight before she vanished.

Leaf closed his eyes now to get a vision of

Poto underwater. *A solid wash of the color blue. Then, the rocky floor of the pond.* Leaf thought he saw Poto, but without warning the scene turned black. It was not Poto that he saw at all. It was the same disturbing vision he had been having the past few days. *Thick, dark ooze clogged the veins of the mountain, like a bad case of cholesterol. A tangled dark web surrounded him. He was trapped.*

He shook his head quickly to dispel the vision. It was horribly unsettling. He had to remind himself that he was standing safely on the sunny bank of Poto's pond. Besides, tonight was the weekly Earth-Guard action meeting. They were going to talk about testing Pockets' carbon-air-earth regulator, or as Pockets called it "the Carthulator". It would be a good time to tell everyone about his ominous visions. They needed to be on the lookout.

"Hey, Poto!" Leaf called. "I'm going back up to Dancing Oak."

Poto popped her head above the water.

"Okay. Catch ya later."

Leaf readjusted his saxophone over one shoulder. He stepped onto his Bramble Mat, then thought better of trying to fly uphill again. He had eaten enough dirt for one day. So, he rolled up the Bramble Mat, prickly side in. He slung it over his other shoulder and walked back up to Dancing Oak.

23

The Water Talks

CHAPTER 8

An Earth-Guard Adventure

POTO WATCHED LEAF WALK away, then glanced at the sun. It looked like it was sitting on the topmost mountain peak. That meant there was at least two more hours of daylight. Two more hours to be at the pond. Great.

"Poto's Pond" was near the bottom of the mountain. It was fed by one of the many streams that ran down the mountain's velvet green hillsides. A thick spray of water fronds grew on its uphill side and sheltered two little waterfalls that flowed over a rocky bank. A carpet of lush, sweetly smelling grass bordered the downhill side of the pond.

Poto slid quietly beneath the surface of the water. Though it had taken time to get used to her tail, she could already do spirals, somersaults and even double underwater backflips. Shimmying close to the rocky bank, she twirled with the bubbles that danced in from the waterfalls. Then, she did a twisting jump straight up, pirouetted once in the air, curved her body in a wide arc and dove down again.

Poto was happiest in the water. Water was like the blood coursing through her veins. Riding the currents felt as easy as sinking into a big featherbed mattress. To become a mermaid is exactly the superpower she would have wished for, and it had happened without her wishing for it first.

The pond was Poto's favorite place on the mountain. Her second favorite place was Bright Lake at the top of Far-and-Yonder-Road. Tall trees surrounded Bright Lake and the air always smelled like pine. It was not as cozy as the pond, but it was wilder and had a bigger personality. Bright Lake's water was so deep that it sometimes had waves, though on still days, the sunlight lay across it like a slather of melted butter.

Poto felt like lazing around on the shore of the pond. She loosened her cape from around her body. Her tail began to disappear and her teal-colored scales changed back to human peach-fuzz. She scrambled out of the pond, now on two legs, and lay on her stomach on the soft grass. The water was like mirrored glass today and skimmer bugs glided haphazardly across the smooth surface.

She made funny faces in the water's reflection laughing when her silly smiles broke into gentle ripples. The water cooed. Not only could Poto become a mermaid, she could hear water speak. She could talk with it. Not in words exactly. But, she knew what it was saying all the same.

Wait! What was that? She heard a faint voice from inside the water. Like a cry. Where was that coming from? She listened more carefully.

"Tell me again," she whispered to the pond and put her face even closer to the water. There was only the giggling of the waterfalls. A few more minutes went by. She knew she had heard something and she needed to hear it again. "Come on, Pond," Poto coaxed, "You said something. Tell me again."

Yes! There it was. This wasn't a giggle. This was more of a groan.

"That is a very unnatural sound for water, " Poto thought.

There was another groan...and then another...then she knew. It was coming from Bright Lake. It was in trouble. Bright Lake was in pain. The groan grew louder. "Oh my," Poto whispered to herself. She could feel the pressure of her heart pounding all the way in her ears. Something strange was going on at Bright Lake. The sound grew louder and more anguished. Poto could not bear it. Without hesitating, she wrapped her cape around herself and slid back into the water. Once again a mermaid, she swam as fast as she could from stream to stream upwards toward Bright Lake.

Leaf Practices Seeing

CHAPTER 9

An Earth-Guard Adventure

LEAF WALKED THE LONG path up the mountain and over one low crest to Dancing Oak. He had tried to fly a few more times, but each time, all he did was fall off of the Bramble Mat. This superpower stuff was supposed to be easy, wasn't it? He still had to work on his Bramble Mat skills and he still had to build his ability to "see". It was like he had two more instruments to practice.

However, he wanted to be able to fly anywhere and he especially wanted to get good at "seeing", so he was determined to do the work. He sat down beneath Dancing Oak and closed his eyes.

It was great whenever he got it right. He only had to sit still and concentrate on a place, and then a vision would appear. One of the challenges, though, was that he was not able to do anything else when he was having a vision. He became completely immobile. He would not be able to escape if danger approached, so he had to be careful how and when he used this power.

This was Leaf's fifth try. He had just "looked in" on Poto and saw her making funny faces at the water.

"She can be so ridiculous," he thought.

He closed his eyes again. He wanted to check in on the other Earth-Guards. He knew he could find Pockets in the Quantum Cave. That was the cave where Old Man Log lived. Pockets had figured out how to tap enough power from the roots to run his computers, so he set up his workspace there. Leaf concentrated and a vision appeared. *Pocket's eyes were iridescent gold as he stared at the glowing screen of his computer. "Yes, fabulistic !" he cried using one of his made-up words. The vast network of tangled roots surrounded him. They held all sorts of wires, widgets and computer chips that Pockets used for his quantum networks and mechanical contraptions.*

Pockets' Carbon-Water-Earth regulator was making an annoying chirping sound. The "Carthulator" was his new invention to help get pollutants out of the air and stabilize global temperatures. It was not working quite right yet. He had also developed a new proton protein Yummy-Matter-Maker that would produce his favorite food instantly. The Yummy-Matter-Maker was working perfectly.

"Macaroni and Cheese!" Pockets said, "How superific."

"Good old Pockets," thought Leaf.

Next, Leaf turned his attention to Nimble. Ah...there he was. *In the Rumbleshed near Criggy Craggy Rock. He had an intent look on his face as he tinkered on his flybercycle. The silver wheels shone and the fenders were polished so bright they sparkled. Directly behind the seat was the black and violet canister that held the power supply.*

The flybercycle was the first of its kind. Its wheels were made from quartaine, a substance that allowed them to spin extra fast. The power supply was Nimble's brand new blasto-rod.

Nimble was on his back fixing the zow-punch throttle. *"Ow!" he yelled accidentally dropping a wrench on his head.* Nimble was super strong and usually agile, but he had been having trouble holding onto his new wrench. Leaf laughed as he watched Nimble fumble a few more times before being able to grab the wrench and hold it tightly.

The sun was touching the third highest peak of the mountain and the air was getting a little cooler. One hour of sunshine left. Leaf would finish by focusing in on Zohna and her horse Mercury. There they were as usual, lounging near Dandelion Crossing, talking. Mercury understood everything Zohna said, and Zohna understood everything Mercury thought. That was how they conversed.

Zohna was talking excitedly about the day. Not only had they discovered a new spider web at Curious Cave, but they had beat Nimble in a race. "Nice work, Merc," said Zohna, chewing lazily on a weed. Mercury was working on a dinner of carrot sandwiches--his favorite meal.

31

"Hey Mercury, my Trusty Red Steed," Zohna said playfully, "You wanna go to Moving Meadows tomorrow? Betcha the knoll has moved a whole ten meters uphill."

Mercury looked at her, a gentle whiny vibrating his soft nostrils as if to say, "You're on." Then, he turned back to his carrot sandwich and took another bite.

Leaf liked the taste of freshly baked tomato pie. "Cold carrot sandwiches," he thought. "Ew. No way."

Poto's In Trouble

CHAPTER 10

An Earth-Guard Adventure

POTO SWAM FROM STREAM to stream winding up the mountain past Lizard's Lair and the Misty Woods, and then alongside The-Far-and-Yonder-Road. She finally reached Bright Lake. There was a strange silence. She listened as hard as she could. There were no sounds. No bird calls. No leaves rustling in the breeze. Nothing.

"Talk to me, Lake," Poto whispered. "Talk to me."

She heard the same faint groaning she had heard at the pond. Poto continued to swim through the Lake. It was eerie. The trees on shore seemed to be sagging. There was a gray cloud cover. There was never any cloud cover at Bright Lake. Something was not right. There were no fish either. Usually, she played and laughed with the fish here. Not today.

Poto kept swimming. Small green bubbles were coming toward her. They looked slimy and sticky. The water was getting thicker and thicker. More bubbles floated her way. These were bigger, greener, slimier, and stickier than the others. They smelled bitter and sharp, like rotten eggs and sour cheese together.

"Oh no. What is this?"

Green bubbles of all sizes began to surround her, some were floating in clumps, others were clinging to her scales and blocking her way forward.   They stung a little as they touched her.   She was frightened and wanted to turn back, but she had to find out what these nasty things were and where they were coming from. It was obvious they were the reason that Bright Lake was in pain.

"Oyster Up" she said to herself.   That was something her grandfather had always said when he wanted her to have courage.   Poto did not know exactly what it meant, but saying it made her less frightened. She pushed toward the middle of the lake to see what she could discover. She was getting weaker and weaker. Each tail stroke became more difficult.   Her body felt sluggish and heavy, and now she could barely move her arms.   Poto grew fainter and gasped for air until she felt she just...couldn't... go on. She needed help. How could everything have gotten so bad so quickly?

MEANWHILE, LEAF WAS TESTING himself on how well he could switch locales. He focused on Nimble at the Rumbleshed, then on Pockets in the Quantum Cave and then back to Nimble. He checked in on Zohna and Mercury at Dandelion Crossing, then switched to Pockets and once more to Nimble. So far, so good.

It had been awhile since he had looked in on Poto, so he switched his attention to Poto's Pond. Hmmm. He was having trouble finding her. Leaf concentrated harder and shut his eyelids even tighter. He finally got a view of the pond. Great.

"Now," he thought, "Where's Poto?"

He checked beneath the water. No Poto. He looked around the shoreline. No Poto. He scanned the rock where she likes to sit. No Poto. "She must be there somewhere, " he thought. "This seeing stuff can be so temperamental." Leaf was frustrated.

He quieted himself and looked again. Still no Poto.

"Maybe she went to Bright Lake," he thought. "She likes it there, too, but it's so late in the day. Still...maybe."

Leaf hoped he was right. It would be better to find her at Bright Lake than to face the fact that his seeing ability was not getting as good as he thought. He switched his gaze to the top of the Far-and-Yonder-Road. It was hard to get that vision into focus.

Everything was blurry. It seemed cloudy for some reason. Leaf re-calibrated the color tuning in his head. Aha. *Teal-colored skin.* He kept looking. Yes, there she was. He definitely saw teal-colored skin. But, wait. *There was no movement and the skin was covered in some kind of slimy green bubbles.* Leaf opened his vision wider. *A blue-green tail was dragging below the surface.* Oh no! There she was. It was Poto. *She wasn't moving. She was just floating there surrounded by slimy green bubbles all different sizes.* What were those? Where did they come from? "Oh no!" thought Leaf. "That was Poto and she wasn't moving."

Rush To Bright Lake

CHAPTER 11

An Earth-Guard Adventure

NIMBLE WAS THE FIRST to hear the saxophone call. It was Leaf. Leaf played his saxophone to round up everyone for strategy talks or brainstorming sessions. But, this was not the gathering call. This was "Bop-de-bop-bop-booooo-bip-bip!" It was the alarm and it meant, "Come at once!" Nimble put down his tools, carefully this time. Ready or not, it was time to try out the flybercycle for increased speed. He had been working on getting it to go 200 miles per hour. His dream was to get it up to 1,000 miles per hour, though he would have to develop a new helmet before he could ride it that fast. Nimble swung his leg over the seat, powered it up and jetted away from Criggy Craggy Rock.

POCKETS DOUBLE-CHECKED his computer code. Hmmm...something wasn't right. There was an odd sound that was kind of blaring and soulful. Had he programmed that in? He thought he had decided on a refined digital "bing". Wait, it wasn't coming from his computers at all. It was Leaf's saxophone. Pockets carefully saved his calculations, minimized the size of his plasma graphs and placed them in the "in-progress" wedge of his quantum organizer. When Leaf called, that meant something important was happening. Mac and cheese would have to wait. Pockets went outside to be ready when Nimble showed up. That's how they did it. In a second, Nimble swooped by on his flybercycle,

"Hey, Quantum kid, get the lead out," said Nimble, "Leaf called."

Pockets joked, "I was out here before you even powered up that old clunker of yours." Then he added in a serious tone, "Something feels very wrong. Let's get there fast."

"You bet," said Nimble.

Pockets climbed onto the back of the flybercycle and the two raced up to Dancing Oak.

ZOHNA LOOKED UP WITH a start when she heard Leaf's sax. She quickly picked up her cowboy hat from where it lay on the ground next to her. She pushed the hat down on her head and scrambled to her feet.

"Mercury," she said quickly, "Dinnertime is over."

Mercury stopped in mid-chew, eyes bright, ears forward and raised his proud red roan head. In a flash, Zohna swung herself up onto his back and turned him toward Dancing Oak. They took off like the wind.

NIMBLE AND POCKETS ARRIVED FIRST. The flybercycle had expertly glided over rocks, ridges and hillsides moving faster than a mountain lion chasing down dinner. When Zohna rode up on Mercury, Leaf told them what he had seen.

"Let's go!" Zohna said.

Leaf climbed onto Mercury's back. He realized now, more than ever, how important it was for him to learn to fly uphill on his Bramble Mat. Nimble gunned the flybercycle and they all took off for Bright Lake.

The Dirty Guys Are Discovered

CHAPTER 12

An Earth-Guard Adventure

THE EARTH-GUARDS RACED up the side of the mountain, beneath the Chirping Crags, and across Thornridge Hill to the top of The-Far-and-Yonder Road. When they reached the Lake, they were horrified at what they saw. Poto was lying in the murky green water. Her tail drooped beneath the surface. She was covered with slimy bubbles. Her head was face down in the water. She was very still. Then, Leaf saw her arm move very slightly.

"She's barely breathing, but she's alive," Leaf said urgently.

"Hold on, Bubble Tail," Zohna said as she grabbed a lasso from Mercury's saddle. "We're here."

Zohna threw the rope gently around Poto and pulled her limp body ashore. She took some herbs from her saddlebags and mixed them with water from her canteen to create a poultice. Zohna studied the healing powers of plants and always carried some with her. She applied it to Poto's face and neck. Poto began to breathe a little more deeply

"Whew!" Zohna was relieved. "That was too

41

close for comfort."

Pockets jumped off of the flybercycle. "I'll check the composition of the bubbles in the Lake."

He ran to the lake's edge, shook his arm and his Enviro-meter shot out from under his sleeve. He tested the bubbles.

"It's bleach, plastiscene, RDT, MLH, ethyl-prion, and a concoction of distillates. Basically, poison. It must have killed all the fish, too. Poto is lucky to be alive! This is one sick lake."

"How'd it get there?" Nimble asked. Pockets shook his head.

Leaf felt the prickles of his Bramble Mat against his back. He wanted to fly away. He wanted to play his saxophone loud and harshly. He wanted to...well...the truth was he didn't know what to do. He had not protected Poto and something rotten was happening on Earth-Guard Mountain. Leaf's eyes squinted and his voice sounded lower than usual,

"Someone did this and we're going to find out who it was," he said.

"But, how?" Zohna asked.

Everyone looked at Leaf and waited for him to come up with a plan. Not knowing where to begin, he did the only thing he could think of and sunk into a trance. He began to scan the mountain to see what he could see. *Trees. Mountain peaks. The setting sun. Then suddenly dark-*

ness. Just darkness everywhere. Once again, Leaf thought his seeing ability wasn't working. He shook his head in frustration, blinked twice and closed his eyes again. *Still darkness, but suddenly there was a gentle flash of light. Then darkness again. Then light. Darkness, light, darkness, light.* Someone was traveling through a forest. This was the sunlight coming through the trees as the traveler passed beneath them. Leaf sank deeper into his trance and the image became clearer. *There was a large man, almost as round as he was tall, dressed from head to foot in gray. He drove a big black machine. It had four slate black wheels. A long pointed hood jutted way out in front of the car and was held up by one small, red wheel at the very front. The car had a rough-looking exterior as if it were made of millions of small sharp metal pieces fused together. It rattled as it sped and spewed huge clouds of black smoke. The driver's eyebrows were so thick and long that they joined in the middle to make one long hairy line that went clear across his forehead. He had a twisted smile on his face.*

Leaf's face began to twitch. The other Earth-Guards knew that when Leaf's face twitched he was having a potent vision. They waited anxiously to find out the identity of the culprit who had poisoned Bright Lake and nearly killed Poto. Leaf was still deep in the trance of his vision.

Next to the large man, there was a tall woman.

43

She had rough, jet black hair that fell in a tangled mess to her waist. She had a beaked nose and angry eyes. They were traveling in silence.

Leaf opened his eyes. "It's Onebrow Care-not and Only Mee, two of the notorious Dirty Guys Old Man Log warned me about."

Zohna jumped up, "Oh, my gosh. They must be on their way to continue with some toxic plot."

"Great!" said Nimble "Our first mission. And, they've come to us."

"I bet they have a hideout near here," said Pockets. "Why else would they be coming to the Mountain?"

Leaf answered, "They're traveling through the Dark Woods. Zohna, you stay here until Poto feels like herself again. Then, the two of you can come quickly on Mercury. Nimble, Pockets, come with me. Let's find out where they've been hiding."

Leaf and Pockets climbed onto the back of Nimble's flybercycle and sped away.

The Hideout

CHAPTER 13

An Earth-Guard Adventure

NIMBLE, POCKETS AND LEAF raced through Rattlesnake Ravine and alongside Speaking Creek. They zoomed past Scary Gorge and then to the top of Coyote Cliff. They were headed in the direction of Leaf's vision—toward the Dark Woods on the far side of the mountain. They knew this entire mountain, but none of them had ever been to the top of Coyote Cliff before. None of them dared even to think about the Dark Woods.

When they reached the clifftop, Nimble stopped the flybercycle. Wow. Look at that. They could see the entire mountainside from here. The setting sun cast a strange light on the land. There was a little chill in the air. The dust from the day was settling and everything felt very still. The first crickets began to chirp.

"There it is," Pockets said in an unsteady whisper. A winding path led down the mountain and disappeared into a thick forest. "There's the Dark Woods."

"Keep your pockets on," said Leaf. "We're not going to let a little fear stop us."

"Who says I'm afraid?" Pockets objected trying to hide the shake in his voice. "I'm bravarageous."

"OK, right," Leaf humored him.   "Nimble, let's go!"

Before long, they were entering the Dark Woods.

"Which way?" Nimble asked. "I can smell the exhaust from their car, but I can't tell which direction they went."

Leaf could only use his power to "see" when he was not moving and he didn't want to stop now and slow their progress.

"Turn on the night vision lamp," he responded. Just as Nimble switched on the light, they caught a glimpse of the dirty guys' car far ahead.

"There they are," smiled Nimble.

The three Earth Guards sped through the darkness in pursuit of Onebrow Care-not and Only Mee. Nimble masterfully guided the flybercycle around misshapen tree roots that curled in and out of the ground. He dodged low-hanging branches that hung thickly with rough leaves. There was a musty, wet smell all around them. Small, shadowy animals darted here and there across the path. An owl hooted and a bat flew within inches of their heads. Every so often the night vision head lamp would reflect off the jagged black exterior of that smoke-spewing vehicle zooming away far in front of them.

"We're on the right track," said Leaf. "It

won't be long now."

Pockets held on and kept his eyes closed. They were going fast and speeding through the darkness made him cold. Pockets hated to be cold.

As they came out of the Dark Woods, the road turned sharply and they all leaned into the curve as Nimble accelerated. Ah! Now they would be right on the tail of Onebrow and Only Mee. Yet, once around the curve, there was no trace of the two filthy criminals. They had disappeared.

Nimble was mystified, "How'd they do that?"

"Oh no." Pockets sighed.

"We'd better stop," Leaf said.

Nimble slowed up the flybercycle until it came to a full stop. Now Leaf could try to get a vision. He closed his eyes. *There was a huge cement door. It opened automatically and the dirty guys drove through the doorway. The door began to slowly swing shut behind them.*

Then Leaf had a second vision. *The door was closing. There was a glimpse of the sun setting on dark green hills.* Aha! He must be looking OUT from INSIDE the doorway. Yes! This was a doorway into the mountain itself.

"They are INSIDE the mountain," Leaf cried. "Let's go. I'll show you."

Inside The Mountain

CHAPTER 14

An Earth-Guard Adventure

NIMBLE PULLED AT THE solid cement door that was fixed into the side of the mountain. He was strong and he was sure that he would have no problem opening it. After several tries, however, the door had not moved.   Nimble shook his head. "It won't budge."

"Knock, knock," said Pockets.

"Aw, come on," said Nimble, irritated, "This is no time for jokes."

"Just answer," said Pockets. "Knock, knock."

"Who's there?" Leaf replied. Leaf liked knock-knock jokes.

"Isador."

"Isador who?" said Leaf

"When Isador NOT a door?"

"That's stupid, Quantum-kid" Nimble complained. "That's not how a knock-knock joke goes."

"Just answer the question." Pockets said. "When Isador not a door?"

"When?" Leaf obliged.

"When it's been dissolved!" Pockets beamed as he reached into his back pocket and took out his Metal Muncher "This can dissolve old metals.

It should have no problem with that cement door!" Pockets sprayed his Metal Muncher on the stubborn door. The three waited as the cold cement began to fizzle. It was working. Pockets figured it would take about sixty seconds for the door to melt away completely. He checked his watch.

"55...54...53," he said. The cement bubbled, melted, popped, hissed, even sparked a few times. "25...24..23...almost done..."

Then everything stopped. No more fizzling. Nothing. Only the very edges of the door had been eaten away. Most of it was intact and still barred the way into the mountain.

"Bad news!" said Pockets. "I must have brought the weaker batch."

"It's all I need," said Nimble confidently. "Now I can get a better grip." He grabbed a hold of the disintegrated edge and leaned back. His biceps tightened. He grimaced. His face reddened "Unh! Urg!" He gave his best strong-guy sounds as he pulled. The door still did not budge.

"Come on, Flyber Boy," Leaf needled him. "I thought you were stronger than this." Leaf didn't have another plan and he needed Nimble to succeed.

Nimble leaned back once more, grunted and tugged with more strength than he had ever used before. If he failed in front of Leaf, he would never live it down.

"Hey, Muscles," said Pockets with a sly grin on his face. "Try pushing."

Nimble gave him an irritated glance.

"He's right," said Leaf. "I think it goes the other way."

Nimble dropped his hands for a second and breathed out heavily, exasperated with himself. Then, he re-set his feet into a solid stance. He inhaled sharply, exhaled hard and rammed his shoulder against the door. "Unnhhh." The door let out a grinding creak like an old man's hacking cough and opened wide.

"There!" Nimble laughed. "I knew what I was doing all the time." Pockets and Leaf looked at each other and rolled their eyes.

The three approached the doorway cautiously and peered inside. They saw a long hallway that disappeared into the mountain. They glanced at each other and nodded. Nimble got back onto the flybercycle and started it up. Pockets and Leaf climbed on behind him. They drove slowly into this strange place. Leaf was not sure how they would do it, but he was determined to put an end to the dirty doings of Onebrow Care-not and Only Mee.

The Dirty Guys

CHAPTER 15

An Earth-Guard Adventure

"STOP HEEERE. MR. CARE-NOT," said Only Mee. Her words stretched out in a breathy, sinister moan.

Onebrow stopped the car. They had traveled through a network of subterranean tunnels and were parked on a platform that overlooked a gigantic underground cavern. Only Mee stepped from the car. She walked to the edge of the platform and leaned against the railing.

""Look at Underhall, Mr. Caaare-Not." She gave a dramatic long-armed gesture at the enormous chamber below. "This is my empire."

The chamber was suffused with a chilly, lifeless light from the glow of a hundred dimly lit wall lamps. Doorways of all shapes and sizes were set at varying heights into the cold gray walls. These led to an elaborate network of hidden pipelines and passageways. Everything here had a pale pickle-colored hue from soaking in the fumes of the green toxic bubbles that traveled through this complex underground maze.

"I am in control of everything here." Only Mee bragged. Her boasting only made her more attractive to Onebrow.

53

"Yes, you are in control, my love," he replied with a twinkle in his eye and a voice as coarse as sandpaper.

"I am living a dreeeam," she continued. "And all built on the money I get from concocting a lovely, poisonous bubbling soup."

"You give a new meaning to the term 'Going Green', my love." Onebrow said adoringly.

"It's my service to the world, Mr. Care-not. Everyone wants to get rid of their poisonous run-off. I take it off their haaands and re-direct it to a place no one cares about...like this silly mountain."

"You are brilliant my dear, brilliant." He was becoming more and more enthralled with her.

Only Mee continued, "And, once the Lake is dead, the magic in this mountain will be mine."

Onebrow let out a hyena-like cackle. "Your ambition is as big and beautiful as this pickle green chamber, my sweet. When is the next release?"

As sudden as a harsh slap, Only Mee stiffened, her face darkened and she glared at him. "There was a problem in the Vat laaast time because of YOUR careless measurements. It took me far tooo long to rectify the situation." Just as quickly, she regained her composure and lowered her voice. "All processes are working again. If you do everything right, the bubbles will ferment and coaaagulate and we can releeease them tonight." She shivered with anticipation and burst out with a harsh, bullet-like laugh that echoed against the cold walls.

Onebrow replied, "I will make sure all flow-ways are ready, my lovely."

He held a round, gray controller in his hand. Its glowing screen showed the status of all the areas in the hideout. "Underground Passage-way One is open," Onebrow confirmed and then continued, "Pipes from the Vat Release Room are open. Flow-way to Underground Riv---Wah-hhh?!!" He stopped in mid-sentence.

"Something wrong?" Only Mee was suspicious.

Care-not's eyebrow was raised halfway up his forehead in alarm. The jowls of his cheeks began to quiver as he shook his head in dismay.

"The main doorway has been breached! The main doorway has been breached!" he said, now frantic, his jowls jiggling uncontrollably like old jello.

"Whaaat?!" Only Mee was enraged.

"The door has been violently forced open and...." He looked at her, his eyebrow raised even higher and curved in dread, "...and partially disintegrated!"

"Disintegraaated?" Who did this?" she asked.

Onebrow consulted his controller again and brought up an image of the entrance hall.

"Take a look at this, my love," and he held the controller so she could see. There was Nimble, Pockets and Leaf on the flybercycle.

"It's those self-important Earth-Guards," she said, her words sounding more sinister than ever. Her long hair began to rise on her head. "I knew they would come...just not so soon."

"But, you have a plan for them, don't you, my love?" Onebrow sniggered knowingly.

Only Mee's lips were pursed, her nostrils flared. "Yeeesss," she smiled and began to drum her long fingers together.

"They are like little gnaaats. Bothersome, but when we get a hold of them...," she clapped her hands together sharply, "...they will be squashed."

Onebrow chuckled.

"All of the inner-wall delivery systems aaare working?" she asked

"Yes, my one-and-Only," he replied.

She tossed her head and headed quickly toward the car.

"Let's go," she ordered as she climbed in, "We haaaven't a minute to lose."

"Where are we headed, my love?" Onebrow followed. He jumped into the driver's seat and started up the engine.

"Well, Mr. Care-not, we aren't being very goood hosts, are we? I think our little visitors need a welcoming committeee."

Onebrow snickered as he backed up the car and turned it around. Then, they rumbled down a tunnel toward the main entrance and the unsuspecting Earth-Guards.

The Encounter

CHAPTER 16

An Earth-Guard Adventure

ZOHNA REMOVED THE HERBAL poultice. It had worked. Poto was slowly regaining consciousness.

"Hey...Poto," Zohna whispered.

Mercury nudged her gently. Poto welcomed the feeling of Mercury's soft nose. She opened her eyes slowly and looked at Zohna. Her vision was still dazed and blurry. Her voice was small and weak. She felt parched and her body ached.

"What happened?"

"You were poisoned by the water in the Lake." Zohna replied.

Mercury snorted his disgust at the thought of what had happened to Bright Lake.

"Leaf, Nimble and Pockets went to find who did this," said Zohna. "We need to follow them. Do you feel well enough to ride?"

Poto's eyes were growing brighter. She felt her cheeks flush. There was a warm tingling in her arms and legs.

"I'm ready," she said.

Zohna climbed onto Mercury's back and then helped Poto up. Mercury threw his head back, red mane wild, and eyes dancing. He neighed loudly and sped off.

THE FLYBERCYCLE'S TIRES MADE rubbery sounds on the floor of the long hallway as Nimble, Pockets and Leaf drove slowly into the mountain. They looked with uneasiness at what surrounded them. Everything was gray cement. There was a gray cement floor, gray cement walls and a gray cement ceiling. There was a double row of buzzing, sputtering fluorescent lights overhead. It went on for a very long way.

"Stop again," Leaf directed Nimble. Leaf tried to get a vision of something that would provide a clue to the whereabouts of Only Mee and Onebrow Care-not, but nothing came. Pockets was getting cold again.

"This is way too coldiferous for me," Pockets said.

"Shhh," warned Leaf, "Let's keep going. Everyone be on the lookout."

Nimble continued slowly down the corridor. They traveled for several minutes, but still nothing about the corridor had changed. Nimble began to drive a little faster.

"What's that smell?" Pockets asked.

There was a sharp, pungent odor in the corridor, like rotten food mixed with gasoline.

"It smells like your Yummy-Matter-Maker when it's on the fritz," Nimble joked. Before

Pockets could think of a retort, the flybercycle began to swerve.

"Hold on," said Nimble, "There's something slippery on the floor. I'm going around it."

Sure enough, a putrid puddle of strange greenish slime was seeping onto the floor from the left side of the hallway. It oozed right through the cement itself and flooded toward the flybercycle. Nimble veered sharply around it.

"That was close," he said. But, more noxious muck threatened them from the other side of the hall. Nimble gunned the cycle to avoid it. Whew! Another narrow escape. Wait. Oh no! The sinister slime lay ahead of them, too.

Nimble turned up the Friction Factor of the tires for better traction. He did his best swerving and veering. Leaf and Pockets held on, shifting their weight as best they could with each tilt and turn. They were almost past the foul fluid when Nimble lost control of the flybercycle. It slid onto its side and careened across the corridor. Nimble, Pockets and Leaf landed with a "wump" on the cold gray floor.

"Ouch!" "Ugh." "Ow!"

They scrambled clumsily to their feet, disoriented and confused. At that moment, a loud, angry buzzer sounded. The buzzer rumbled so intensely that it vibrated their bones. A huge gangplank descended from the ceiling directly in front of where they now stood. As the gangplank lowered, it revealed Onebrow Care-not and Only Mee. They were standing in front of their black car, its smelly smoke still rising in little coughs from the exhaust pipe. With a caustic clack, the edge of the gangplank locked into place against the floor.

"Nice of you to visit our humble abode," Onebrow chuckled, then glanced sideways at Only Mee. "You had some entertainment planned for our visitors, my love?"

"Is everyone comfortable?" Only Mee asked, "I think it's a bit waaarm in here."

Pockets gulped, spun around and began to run away down the corridor. Only Mee blast-ed him with a laserbeam of her icy stare and stopped him cold.

"Pockets!" Nimble cried out.

Then Nimble turned and lunged wildly at Only Mee. She aimed her frozen gaze on him and slowed him down in mid-run. By the time he reached her, he was frozen solid.

Leaf half-grabbed, half-fumbled for his saxo-phone. He knew he could blow an ear-shatter-ing blast that might stun her. But Only Mee reached him in two menacing steps of her long legs and swiped the instrument from his hands. She then threw her chin back as if to laugh, but instead violently jerked her head forward. Her long black hair flipped over her head from behind her. As her hair flew, it transformed into an immense snarled net and engulfed Leaf completely. She quickly snapped her head back again and stood up straight. The valiant leader of the Earth-Guards was trapped on top of her head, tangled in the fierce knots of her coarse tresses. She still held his saxophone with one hand. Waving the other hand in the air, Only Mee flicked her long fingers and shouted orders to Onebrow.

"You know what to dooo with those two, Mr. Care-not."

"Yes, my love. Heh. Heh."

"I'm taking this one with me," she said. "He'll get a ringside seat to the greeening of his friend's beloved Lake."

She strode off down another cold cement corridor with Leaf, on top of her head, struggling to get free.

Zohna And Poto In Ugly Underhall

CHAPTER 17

An Earth-Guard Adventure

IT WAS EARLY EVENING and the light of the full moon cascaded across the mountain. It was bright enough for Mercury, Zohna and Poto to follow the flybercycle's tracks to the top of Coyote Cliff and down the other side. They could even follow the tracks through the Dark Woods. Before too long they arrived at the open, partly disintegrated, cement door.

"They're in there," Zohna said.

Mercury snorted.

"Mercury," said Zohna, "You had better wait here in case we need a quick getaway."

Mercury stamped one foot in protest. He wanted to be in on the adventure, but he trusted Zohna's judgment. He stayed outside the cement doorway and watched with big-eyed concern as the two Earth-Guards walked slowly into the mountain, being very wary and watchful.

Zohna led the way. Their footsteps echoed in the dreary grayness of the long corridor. It smelled dank and unnatural. The stale air felt cold and dingy against their skin.

Poto was afraid and kept looking around

nervously. She was usually frightened in enclosed places and this was no different. Leaf and the others had saved her though, and now it was her turn to help them. She thought about the horrible plight of Bright Lake, too, so she was going to keep going even though she shivered with every step. She took a breath to calm herself. After a few more steps, she noticed something sparkling on the cold floor. It shimmered iridescent blue and purple.

"Look!" she called to Zohna.

It was one of Pockets' sensors. He had left it there for them to find.

"They're definitely in here somewhere."

"I knew it," said Zohna. "Let's keep going."

They kept walking for a painfully long time down this endlessly long, gray corridor. Finally, it curved and widened, ending abruptly at the entrance to a gigantic, cavernous room. The room was as round and as big as Couger Canyon and its curved ceiling rose higher than the Chirping Crags. It glowed with a pickle-green light. Staring into this gargantuan room made Zohna and Poto feel like two lost ants. There was a big sign suspended in the middle of the room that said, **Welcome to Ugly Underhall**.

"Ugh," said Zohna. "This must be the place. It sure IS ugly."

There were randomly shaped hatches, gateways and doors all around the big room at many different levels.

"How will we find them?" Poto was frustrated.

"Where's that sensor you found?" Zohna said.

"I left it back in the hallway," answered Poto.

"You left it?" said Zohna, very exasperated. "Well, I don't want to go all the way back there now. They're here somewhere. Let's keep looking."

Each entryway had a sign above it:

Toxins Keep Out   **Development Room**
Dirty Mixing   **Thwarted Plans**   **Escape Route**
The Place We Take Captured Earth-Guards

Zohna pointed, "That one!"

This entryway rose nearly halfway up the wall of the cavern. A large metal gate blocked anyone from entering. It was an old iron gate, with spires on top and a rust-covered handle toward the bottom.

"Ew," said Poto. "I don't even want to touch it."

"I'll do it," said Zohna, always the brave one.

She grabbed the handle and pulled. The gate moved an inch and then stopped. Click-clang. It was latched from the other side.

"Can you throw a rope up there?" Poto asked, pointing to the top of the gate.

Zohna hadn't ever thrown a rope that high before. But, her ropes had become magical and she was Zohna, "Self-Reliant Trailblazer". She nodded and reached for one of her lassos from beneath her poncho.   Biting one lip in deep concentration, Zohna unwound the rope and swung it above her head three times. Then she threw it as high as she could.

"Go rope!" she directed.

It stretched out farther and farther. It sailed higher and higher. Finally, it looped securely around a spire on the top of the gate. Zohna yanked it tightly.

"Yes!" she smiled proudly.

"Now make sure it stays firm," said Poto who then grabbed the rope and began to shinny up.

Zohna was amazed.

"How'd you learn to do that?"

"Playing with seaweed in the ocean," Poto yelled from the top of the gate.

Poto climbed over, pulled the rope up with her and slid down the other side. Then she opened the gate for Zohna.

"Great work, Water Girl." Zohna smiled.

The celebration of their success was cut short when they turned to see another very long hallway with more doors all along it on either side. Ugh. They would have to look in every one. Well, if that's what they had to do, that's what they had to do. No matter how long it took, they were determined to find their friends.

The two hurried down the long corridor going

quickly from door to door. When there was a window, they'd peek in. When there was no window, they'd listen intently.

"Do you see anything?" Poto asked.

"No. Do you hear anything?"

Poto shook her head. The two looked at each other, discouraged.

"We have to keep going," Zohna said.

They continued down the hallway, listening at and looking in door after door. They desperately hoped to find any sign of Leaf, Pockets or Nimble.

Nimble Nabber And Virus Vault

CHAPTER 18

An Earth-Guard Adventure

ZOHNA WAS THE FIRST to hear the grumbling voice of Onebrow Care-not.

"No more cycle for you, young man. Here it goes!"

Zohna whispered urgently, "Poto, over here."

Luckily the door was unlocked and the two quietly pushed it open. The scene that greeted them was horrifying. Nimble was trapped inside a round contraption that was walled in by thick glass on all sides. It was labeled *The Nimble Nabber.* On the far side of the room, a chain suspended his flawless flybercycle over a vat of bubbling green goo. There were clouds of steaming gas swirling up from the vat. It smelled AWFUL. Poto gasped. Onebrow had his back to the door and had not seen them yet. Zohna put her finger to her lips and threw a stern look at Poto as a warning to be quiet. It was important that they were not discovered.

Mr. Care-not was flailing his arms around in the air. He was laughing and pointing at the flybercycle as it was being lowered inch by inch toward the bubbling goo. Nimble, angry and distressed, was slapping his hands against the thick glass of The Nimble Nabber trying to get out.

All of a sudden, a rope encircled the flyber-cycle, tightened around its frame and with a "thwap", yanked it free. The cycle flipped over and landed right side up on both wheels next to where Nimble was being held.

"Wahhh?" Onebrow exclaimed in surprise. He turned around to see Zohna holding one end of a magic lasso; the other end was around the cycle. Before he could do anything more, Zohna took out a second rope.

"Go rope!" she commanded.

It sailed through the air, coiled around Onebrow and pinned his arms to his sides.

Zohna commanded, "Rope, take Onebrow to the bubbling goo."

"I won't go. I won't." Onebrow protested as he struggled inside the coiled rope, "And this feeble rope can't make me."

"You'd better release Nimble," Zohna commanded. Her hands were on her hips in an "I-won't-take-no-for-an-answer" stance.

Onebrow laughed. "Never!"

"Then it's goo for you. Go rope!"

The rope grew tighter and dragged Onebrow even closer to the goo. He struggled but he could not get free.

"Tell us how to free Nimble."

"I wouldn't tell you for all the poison messes

in the world."

"Go Rope!" Zohna directed once more.

Onebrow was now an inch from the vat. "I'll never give in," he bellowed.

Zohna and Poto looked at each other not knowing what to do.

"Pockets would know how to free him," Zohna said. Then she turned to Onebrow. "What did you do with Pockets?"

Onebrow laughed, "I've locked him in the Virus Vault. Soon his mind will belong to us."

"The Virus Vault? No!" Poto was frantic. "It'll scramble his thought processes. We have to find him."

"YOU have to go find him," said Zohna. "I need to stay here and make sure Onebrow doesn't escape."

"By myself?" Poto was not sure she could oyster up to this. "How will I do that?"

"Go, Poto," Zohna directed. "Go!"

Zohna did not use too many words, but the words she used were powerful and she always meant exactly what she said. You did not argue with Zohna. Poto knew she had no choice. She inhaled quickly, gave a frightened nod and headed out to look for the Virus Vault.

She continued down the hall past more and more doors. What if she couldn't find Pockets? What if she couldn't free him? Where was Leaf? She needed his help. If only she had remem-

73

bered Pockets' sensor. This is the second time it would have come in handy. Before she could get mad at herself any longer, she saw a blinking sign at the end of the hallway: "Virus Vault." "Virus Vault." "Virus Vault." How lucky. There was no door, either. That was lucky, too. There was only a huge metal threshold and she could simply step over it. Great.

Gaining confidence, Poto ran toward the Virus Vault. She felt bolder knowing she was closer to saving Pockets. As she neared the entryway, she had a gut feeling that she should stop before going through. It's a good thing she did. On the other side of the threshold was a river that flowed sluggishly covered by the same green bubbles that had been in Bright Lake. It passed by her with a gush and glug. She would have been in big trouble if she had fallen in there.

From outside this threshold, she looked across the river and saw a platform. On that platform, tied to little chair...was Pockets. A robotic arm hung in mid-air in front of him. It was holding something strange and dangerous in its metal claw, and the claw was moving closer and closer to his head. He stared at it, eyes wide and terrified.

" Pockets!" screamed Poto.

Leaf Is Trapped

CHAPTER 19

An Earth-Guard Adventure

ON THE OTHER SIDE of Ugly Underhall, Only Mee was standing over Leaf. He had tumbled out of the long, tangled net of her hair. He had landed on the cold, gray floor in the far corner of what seemed to be a control room. The room was as long as Rattlesnake Ravine and twice as tall as Dancing Oak. The wall at the far end was covered in monitor screens that displayed digital and holographic read-outs. There were a lot of clicking and beeping sounds. The other three walls were empty and bare.

Only Mee was still clutching Leaf's saxophone. Her long and pointed fingers curved around the keys like a bird of prey clutching its catch. She tapped the keys with a sinister rhythm.

"What is this thing? Is this how you plaaay it?"

She bit down on the mouthpiece. A horrible squawk emanated from the horn that sounded as if the instrument was in pain. Leaf cringed. It was more than he could take.

"What's wrong little man?" she said, "You don't like my plaaaaaying? It's a song called

'Earth-Guards Won't Cause Me Trouble Anymore'."

Leaf ran at Only Mee to grab the saxophone, but she thrust it into her tangled hair and tossed her head. The saxophone sailed into the air. The strap caught on a hook that was in the ceiling high above them. Leaf stared in horror as his saxophone dangled there far out of his reach.

"You won't be able to uuuuuse that to call your friends now," Only Mee sneered.

At that moment, a frenzied alarm rang from across the room. One of the screens displayed a dizzying dance of blue and puce colored lights. Only Mee's eyes widened in excitement and she whipped her head around to see what was happening. Then, she strode on her long legs to the console of blinking lights and surveyed the sensors.

"It begins." She laughed loudly throwing her head back and tossing her ragged black hair.

Leaf closed his eyes to see what else he could see. *Two doors. A sign on each door. One said,* **Control Room** *The other said* **Release Room** *Inside the Release Room, there was a gigantic reservoir nestled into the floor.*

Thick ooze in the reservoir was gurgling with green bubbles. The bubbles floated to the surface, disappeared, formed again, glommed on to each other, then burst and spilled over the sides onto the floor. A sign on the wall read,

Flow-way to River and Lake *A read-out next to it was counting down the time: "10 minutes, 9:59, 9:58, 9:57...".*

It was far too clear to him now. The poison was created in the reservoir. From there, it would travel through pipelines into an underground river that fed directly into Bright Lake. In less than ten minutes, more toxins would be released and the Lake would be harder...or impossible...to save. Then Leaf's vision went blank. He tried again. Nothing.

The fluorescent lights in this room were the brightest lights he had ever seen. There were two long rows of them. They would sputter and buzz, flicker off, then "pop, zzzz" and surge back on again.

Leaf tried to "see" again. Nothing. It must be those lights. They had blinded his mind. What was he going to do now? He tried hard to think of some plan. He tried to "see" again. Still nothing.

"Why are you doing this?" asked Leaf.

"Oh. The little man speeeaks," Only Mee said, peering over her shoulder at him. "None of your business."

Then, she threw back her head with a wild cackle, "Who's got the laaaaast laugh now!"

Leaf was helpless. He couldn't see. He couldn't reach his saxophone to call the others. He felt dazed. Leaf wondered again why Old

Man Log had made him the leader. "I need to see," he said to himself. "I need to see. I need to call the others. I need to see."

It was no use. The fluorescent lights throbbed in his brain. He hung his head, defeated, not knowing how he could stop Only Mee from continuing her toxic tinkering and carrying out her diabolic scheme.

Poto Enters The Virus Vault

CHAPTER 20

An Earth-Guard Adventure

POTO WANTED TO TURN and run from the green bubbling river, but she knew that she had to save Pockets. She took a deep breath and whispered to herself, "Oyster up". Then, she looked around to see if there was a way to get across. There! A thin ledge ran along the inside of the Virus Vault wall. It led to an open metal aqueduct that curved over the river and ran past the platform where Pockets was tied-up. The aqueduct was labeled "Untoxicated Water". That must be where the clean water from the Lake comes in before the dirty guys toxify it. Poto stepped carefully over the metal threshold of the Virus Vault and tiptoed along the ledge. At the aqueduct, she wrapped her cape around herself. Fusing with her body, it became a tail, as she metamorphosed into a mermaid. She then dove into the aqueduct and swam as fast as she could over the green bubbling river. As she crawled onto the platform, her tail transformed back into legs, and she ran to Pockets.

"Quick," Pockets said, "There's an infected nanobot on that arm. They are going to implant my brain with synaptic interrupter viruses. I

79

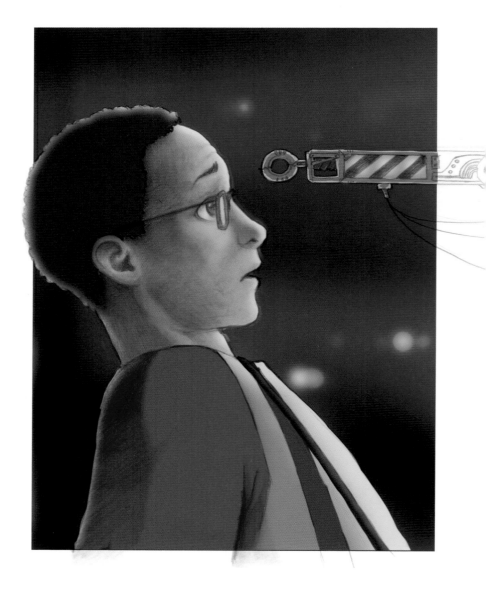

won't be able to think straight. You have to stop it."

"But how?" Poto was frantic.

Pockets' eyes were growing wider as the nanobot got nearer.

"See if there's an emergency override. It should be half-way up the arm."

Poto quickly approached the side of the robotic arm.

"There IS something here," she said.

She saw a small, metal device attached to the side of the arm. She read the words that were printed beneath it. "Laser Beam Shooter for Disabling Arm in Case of Changes in Strategy."

"That's it!" said Pockets. "Pull it off the arm."

"Got it," Poto said.

"There's a nanoscope on the side of it." Pockets continued, "Look through it to locate the nanobot."

"Yes!" said Poto excitedly. "I see it. I see it."

"Fire!" Pockets directed.

Poto didn't move.

"FIRE!" he said urgently.

Poto began trembling but made no other move.

Now Pockets was yelling, "FIRE! POTO! FIRE!"

Finally Poto let out a frightened yell and pressed the trigger control. A laser beam shot out toward the nanobot. "Vsssssszzzzzptttt." The beam missed the arm completely.

The infected nanobot with its synaptic viruses was now just two millimeters from Pockets' forehead. Poto aimed again and fired. "Vsssssszzzz-ppptttt! POP." She hit the edge of the arm. It shattered and a piece of it went flying.

"Ow!" said Pockets. "Something hit me."

He didn't have time to wonder what it was. His full attention was on the nanobot, which was now just an igno-micrometer away from him. Pockets' eyes were wide and his lower lip was quivering.

"IT'S AT MY FOREHEAD. IT'S AT MY FORE-HEAD," he yelled. "TRY AGAIN! POTO! NOW!"

"Vsssszzzzzppppttttttt!."

"Bull's-eye!" said Poto triumphantly.

The robotic arm fizzled into a cloud of blue smoke and fell in a dust shower to the floor.

"I did it," Poto whispered to herself, proud and relieved.

Pockets gasped, "That was too close. My brains were almost mushified."

"Come on," said Poto. "We have to save Nimble."

She untied Pockets from the chair and they ran across the platform back to the aqueduct.

"But I can't swim," said Pockets.

"Don't worry," Poto replied. "Just hold onto me when I become a mermaid and you'll be fine.

That's how it works with mermaids."

Pockets was not so sure. Poto saw the uncertainty in his eyes and smiled, "Trust me."

Sure enough, Pockets held onto Poto and they swam easily to the other side.

They stepped onto the little ledge, and Poto's tail quickly changed back again into feet. She was getting good at that.

"I'm all wet," Pockets complained.

"You'll dry off soon enough," said Poto.

As they crossed over the threshold and out of the Virus Vault, Nimble roared up on his flybercycle.

Poto was surprised to see him.

"You're free!"

"Great news, huh?" said Nimble "Turns out Mr. Care-not is vain about his eyebrow. Zohna's magic rope pulled him so close to the goo that his eyebrow melted away. He cried like a baby and told Zohna how to free me."

"Where is Zohna now?" said Pockets.

"Still watching Onebrow, or should I say NObrow" Nimble answered. "Hey, Quantumkid, you're all wet."

"Yeah...yeah..." said Pockets.

"And there's blood on your forehead. What happened?"

Pockets touched his hand to his head, felt the little cut, then wiped away the blood. "I don't know," he answered. "Doesn't hurt."

83

"OK, hurry up then. Both of you. Get on." said Nimble. "We need to find Leaf."

Leaf Tangles With Only Mee

CHAPTER 21

An Earth-Guard Adventure

THE DANCING LIGHTS OF the monitor flickered across the face of Only Mee. She was anxiously waiting for the toxin release. It was only minutes away. Leaf was on the other side of the room, slumped against the wall, his head hanging. His saxophone was out of his reach. The glaring fluorescent lights had disarmed his vision. He was physically no match for Only Mee and her treacherous net-like hair. He felt empty.

"Some things are only dangerous when you don't know how to use them." He heard a strong, gentle voice speak.

What was that? Leaf looked around to see if the voice was coming from somewhere in the room, but there was no one else there. Then he heard it again.

"Some things are only dangerous when you don't know how to use them."

It was Old Man Log. He was hearing the voice of Old Man Log. How was that possible? What did it mean? Then he remembered. That is what Old Man Log had said when he showed Leaf the Bramble Mat beneath the twisted roots.

The Bramble Mat! Leaf had forgotten that he had it. The still, steady voice spoke again.

"If you trust your power, you own your power."

That was the second instruction. Now Leaf knew that there was a way out of this. The Bramble Mat was still rolled up on his back. He quietly reached for it, and let it slowly unfurl. Then he climbed on and whispered the command.

"We fly!"

Leaf sailed up to his saxophone and lifted it gently from the hook where it had been dangling.

A bell signaled that the polluting goo would be released in three minutes. Only Mee laughed again. Her eyes were aflame with the thrill of anticipation.

"I love watching this," she said and stared with deep, evil joy at the screen. The readout was ticking down and the bubble level was rising. She was completely engrossed in her toxic celebration and unaware of what was taking place behind her.

Leaf blew the Earth-Guard call. "Bop-de-bop-bop-booooo-bip-bip!" Startled, Only Mee turned around. Before she could get a grip on the situation, Leaf did a swooping whoosh and flew straight toward her. She fell back against the control panel and accidentally hit the power command for the room lights. The angry fluorescent lights shut down completely. Ha! Leaf liked the way things were turning out. Literally. Now his power to "see" was back. But, first he would have to finish with Only Mee.

In the semi-darkness, she lunged for Leaf, but he circled around her and banked sharply. She whirled fast to follow him, but lost her balance again and fell on the hard cement floor.

"Wow," thought Leaf. He was impressed with himself. "I've never been able to do that before."

His confidence was coming back. He flew closer to the monitors to see if he could find a shut-off control for the toxin release. But, Only Mee was up all too soon. She grabbed Leaf with both hands and stuffed him back into her knotted hair, Bramble Mat, saxophone and all. Trapped again.

Escape?

CHAPTER 22

An Earth-Guard Adventure

"WHAT'S THAT?" ASKED NIMBLE, "Listen. It's Leaf's saxophone."

"Yes, it certain-lutely is," Pockets said.

"I can zero in on the coordinates with my flybercycle's GPS," said Nimble.

Nimble, with Pockets and Poto on his cycle behind him, raced down the cement hall. He turned left at a big sign that said:

This is What We Dirty Guys Live For

Now they were in a corridor that went deeper into the mountain. The air was stagnant, stinky, and so thick it was hard to breathe. They heard a scuffle from inside a door just ahead of them. All of a sudden, the door swung open. Only Mee was standing there with Leaf in her hair. Nimble gunned his flybercycle and flew right by her. He was hoping to knock her down. Instead, she whirled around and grabbed Poto with one of her long arms. Then she leveled her icy stare at Nimble and Pockets.

They had been frozen once before, and Pockets wasn't about to let it happen again. He reached into his side pocket for his Graphene Radar Razor. He held it high and with one, well-aimed radar beam sheared off Only Mee's hair. Leaf tumbled to the floor.

"My hair!" Only Mee cried. She dropped Poto and clasped her hands to her head. Short, tiny nibs of hair were all that was left of her once thick black netting. "Argh!" she screamed and turned her icy stare away.

"Come on," Nimble said, "Let's get out of here."

"Wait," said Leaf, "The toxic bubbles will be released in less than two minutes. We have to stop it. The chemical mess is stored in a reservoir right next door to this room. Any ideas?"

"Since you asked," said Nimble proudly, "Pockets and I have been working on a toxin neutralizer. I bet it can invade their entire system."

"It was my idea," Pockets said.

"It doesn't matter whose idea it was as long as it works," said Leaf. "Go do it."

"My hair! My hair!" Only Mee was yelling. Still in shock and clutching her head, she ran from the room. Her snarled, de-headed hair slithered along the floor and followed her out.

"I can't say I'm sad to see her go!" said Leaf. "She's such a...."

"Frozen-cistic Diva," Pockets answered.

"Yeah," said Leaf, and shivered.

"POUR THE REST OF IT IN," Nimble directed

Pockets.   They had gone next door and were standing next to the reservoir dropping in their toxin neutralizer. "Let's put an end to this gross gurgling gunk."

Some of the bubbles began to dissipate and dissolve into nothingness. However, new ones still formed, popping and burping out their gross gasses.

"Not so fast, " Pockets warned.

"It's working,"   Nimble said impatiently. "Pour the rest of the crystals in. We don't have much time."

"No. It is not fully conflaburgated yet."

"What does that mean?"

"Conflaburgated.   It's my new word.   It's when .0255 milligrams per power point of crystal solidifies with the urgent liquid spectrum of the designated clean-up target."

"Yeah, yeah, whatever, but...we have to hurry."

"No," Pockets was adamant. "What we have to do is go slowly. This reservoir is deep.   If we don't make sure the job is done right, the bubbles will develop again."

Nimble was too anxious to wait.

"Let me do it," he said.

He hastily grabbed for the vial of crystals, but missed and knocked it out of Pockets' hand. The crystals went flying across the floor of the room.

"Oh no!" breathed Nimble.

They both glanced quickly at the read-out on the wall. Only 59 seconds left, now 58, 57...

"See what you've done," Pockets was angry. "Help me."

The two scrambled around the floor sweeping whatever crystals they could find into the reservoir. The read-out continued its count-down: "20 seconds, 19, 18...". They moved quickly, both hoping that the neutralizer would work even if things were not yet fully "confla-burgated".

There were two seconds left. "One...zero." There was a loud "vroom". The release pump started churning up the poisonous liquid. It then began slurping it out of the reservoir and sending it on its way through the Underhall pipelines. Pockets and Nimble frantically swept the last of the crystals into the reservoir. They held their breath and waited. All of a sudden, the color of the poisonous liquid melted from putrid green to clear blue. There were a few more "pop-pop-pop's", and then the bubbles vanished. The boys let out a sigh of relief and gave each other a "high five".

Their celebration, however, was short-lived for Ugly Underhall gave a violent shake.

"What was that?" asked Nimble.

Another tremor sent them racing for the door, but they weren't fast enough. The door slammed shut in front of them. Nimble tugged on it.

"It's jammed! But, I think I can open it. Just give me a second."

One more jolt made the floor crack and tilt upward. Pockets lost his footing and went tumbling backwards. He fell into the deep reservoir.

"Agh!" he yelled.

Nimble held onto the handle of the Reservoir Release Room door and reached out for Pockets with his other hand. He grabbed Pockets' wrist just in time to keep him from going under and being sucked into the Underhall pipelines by the powerful release pump.

"Don't let go of me," Pockets yelled as he desperately worked to keep his head above the surface of the water. "I can't swim and you're no mermaid."

Nimble didn't dare let go of the door because he might lose his footing and go tumbling after Pockets. And he didn't dare let go of Pockets. He was stuck and stretched between the two. Ugly Underhall shook once more. Nimble's grip on Pockets slipped. Now, he was holding onto only the tips of Pockets' fingers. Pockets was gasping for air.

MINUTES BEFORE, IN THE CONTROL ROOM next door, Leaf opened his eyes from another vision.

"The toxins have been neutralized," he told Poto smiling. "Let's go."

"What was that?" Poto's eyes widened.

They both felt Ugly Underhall shudder and shake. Before Leaf could answer, the same violent tremor that had jammed the door to the Reservoir Release Room, slammed the Control Room door shut, too.

Poto urgently grabbed onto Leaf's arm, "What's going on?"

Leaf closed his eyes and scanned Ugly Underhall. *The pickle-green light in the main cavern was now a soft gold.* Leaf shifted focus. *A sign was blinking: "Virus Vault." "Virus Vault." "Virus Vault." The river just beyond it had turned blue.* He shifted focus again. *The cement walls and ceilings were crumbling everywhere and crashing to the floor.*

"The flow of poisons must have kept Ugly Underhall sturdy," he said. "Now that it has been stopped, the whole place is falling apart."

The next forceful tremor knocked both Poto and Leaf to the floor.

"It's going to collapse," Leaf said.

Poto look at Leaf trying to blink back tears. "Wha--what are we going to do?"

Leaf had no idea how they would escape.

"We Fly"

CHAPTER 23

An Earth-Guard Adventure

POTO WAS TREMBLING. Leaf tried to think of some way out. He scanned the control room for any sign of another exit but saw nothing. He was trying hard to think of another plan when there were a few abrupt bangs from the other side of the door. With a sharp crack, the door flew open. Leaf and Poto were amazed to see Mercury and Zohna. Mercury's nostrils were flaring. Zohna was smiling triumphantly.

"Good boy," she said, patting Mercury's neck. Then she looked at Leaf and Poto, "We found you. Where's Nimble and Pockets?"

"Next door," answered Leaf. "They must be trapped, too."

"I'll be back," she said. In no time, she and Mercury were outside the Reservoir Release Room door.

"Nimble, Pockets," she shouted, "Stand back. We're kicking it in!" Then to Mercury, "Go for it, boy."

"No. Wait!'" Nimble shouted back from the other side. "I can't let go or I may lose Pockets."

"Where is he?" Zohna shouted back.

"He's in the reservoir," said Nimble. "He's

95

slipping away."

Zohna cautioned Mercury, "OK, Boy. Carefully."

Mercury turned his haunches to the door. Using his right hind foot, he hammered the lower portion of the door with a series of small, rapid and well-aimed kicks. He was like a sculptor expertly chipping away at a piece of hard granite. The door moved inward slowly, inch by inch. As it did, Nimble was able to get closer to Pockets. He got a better grip and then pulled Pockets from the churning water in the reservoir. Pockets stood gasping and sopping wet... again.

"OK. We're safe," Nimble said. "Let Mercury go for it." Ugly Underhall trembled once more " ...and fast." he added.

"Take it down." Zohna told Mercury.

With eyes bright and twinkling, Mercury snorted and let loose with a massive kick from both back legs. Clang! The sound reverberated throughout the hallway and the door burst open.

"Bullseye!" said Zohna. Satisfied that Nimble and Pockets were safe, she raced with Mercury back to Leaf and Poto. They were standing outside the Control Room.

"Grab my hand," she said and reached out to Poto.

With one swift motion, Zohna pulled Poto

onto Mercury's back behind her. Leaf climbed onto his Bramble Mat. Nimble and Pockets ran to the flybercycle. The six of them began to zoom out of Ugly Underhall as it rocked and jolted.

The Earth-Guards raced up the long gray corridor. Pieces of concrete fell from the walls around them. One narrowly missed Nimble and Pockets. One fell in front of Mercury but he leapt over it without missing a gallop. Something fell on the back of Leaf's Bramble Mat knocking him onto the cold floor. Leaf closed his eyes for just a second after he fell and a vision appeared. *A tunnel blocked by rubble.* It was the tunnel they had taken here. He shouted, "Turn left at the next corridor."

Nimble looked back from his flybercycle and yelled, "No. We take a right."

"Trust me," said Leaf.

They made a left at the next corridor following Leaf's advice. It's a good thing, too. The right corridor had already collapsed. If they had turned right at the speed they were going, they would have crashed head on into a pile of rubble.

Leaf remounted his Bramble Mat. "We fly!"

He soon caught up with the others. Leaf took the risk of closing his eyes several times. Though traveling at a high speed, he was able to catch sight of where Ugly Underhall had already collapsed. Leaf continued directing the Earth-Guards in a circuitous route back to the surface of the mountain.

Mercury was running at full speed. Nimble kept gunning his flybercycle. Leaf pushed his Bramble Mat faster than he thought possible. Good thing they weren't going any slower because Ugly Underhall was crashing down right behind them. They flew through the doorway that opened to the outside of the mountain just as it creaked loudly and crumbled. A big cloud of gray dust rose into the air. They had escaped, but not a second too soon.

The Earth-Guards stood still and silent, looking in shock at the closed entry now in ruins. The booming and crashing echoed in their heads. Nimble powered-down his flybercycle. He was exhausted, though proud of how well his flybercycle had performed.

Poto felt empty. She slid off Mercury and sat silently on the grass. Leaf's muscles trembled as he stepped from his Bramble Mat and stared motionless at the collapsed door. Zohna leaned forward from her saddle, her arms around Mercury's neck.

"You're the most amazing horse in the entire world," she whispered.

Mercury, breathing hard through flared nostrils, neighed back softly.

"How did he find us?" Poto asked weakly.

Zohna pulled something from Mercury's breastplate. "He found the sensor that Pockets left behind. Good thing you didn't pick it up, Watergirl, or we may not have escaped."

Zohna looked at Pockets and threw him the sensor. He caught it with one hand and held it tightly. They had been underground all night and he lay on the grass in a ray of morning sunshine. Shaking and still wet, he was grateful for its warmth.

They were all reeling with the thought that they had almost been stuck inside forever. It had been a close call.

Then, they heard a simpering sniffle. A short distance away, Onebrow Care-not was sitting in a dejected lumpy heap. He must have escaped the goo and run out of Underhall when it began to collapse. He was panting heavily from having exerted himself and was still coiled inside one of Zohna's ropes.

"What are we going to do with him?" Poto asked.

"Yeah," said Pockets. He's so Publicly Inappropriate."

Nimble replied, "If you ask me, he belongs in a rehab program for the environmentally challenged."

Onebrow caught his breath and looked up to see the Earth-Guards staring at him. He furrowed his bare forehead, now pasty and pale with no eyebrow. With a whimper, he struggled to his feet and took off in an awkward galump toward the Dark Woods.

"He's getting away!" Poto said.

"Don't worry," said Leaf. "I don't think he's dangerous without his precious Only Mee telling him what to do."

"Yeah," said Nimble, "And his beloved goo."

"Where IS Only Mee?" Poto asked.

They all looked quietly at the crumbled doorway. No one answered.

Morning At Bright Lake

CHAPTER 24

An Earth-Guard Adventure

THE EARTH-GUARDS DID IT. They had stopped the toxic green bubbles. They had saved Bright Lake. They had defeated the dirty guys. Now it was time for a little fun.

Nimble, Pockets and Leaf decided to spend a few minutes up on Coyote Cliff. A thin layer of mist hung motionless over the valley, but the morning was becoming a glorious golden. A hawk screeched in the sky. The boys sat there for a good long time.

"I think I can get power from the hawks," Pockets said. "I've been working on a Hawk Scream Collector Conduit."

"Except it does nothing but make a popping sound that scares the hawks away," Nimble kidded him.

"Oh yeah, Flyber-baron," Pockets retorted. "You just wait."

"I'll race you home," Leaf challenged.

"You're on," said Nimble. "There's no way you'll beat my flybercycle, Bramble Boy. Besides, you don't even know how to use that thing."

"Things have changed with me and my Bramble Mat," Leaf answered and then added with a playful taunt, "I trust my power and now I OWN my power."

"Man your machines, gentlemen." Pockets always officiated at any race or competition.

"I've got an idea," said Leaf, "We'll do it in two phases. First to Bright Lake and then to your Rumbleshed."

"Deal."

"On your mark. Get powered. Go!" Pockets declared.

Pockets held on tightly to Nimble as the flyber-cycle sped away. Leaf's Bramble Mat recoiled for a quick second. Then with a "whoosh", it jetted into the sky.

ZOHNA AND POTO RODE Mercury to Bright Lake. It was important for Poto to make sure the Lake was regaining its health. It had already returned to its normal bright blue and the sunshine was beginning to lie like amber honey across the surface. Mercury sipped the cool, clear water after the long journey from Ugly Underhall. Zohna sat at the water's edge, listening to the lap, lap, lap of the waves on the shore. She was chewing on a weed and admiring Mercury's beautiful red roan mane.

Poto wrapped her cape around herself and dived in. This time Bright Lake was healthy, and the water cooed and sighed. The fish were back, too. They gathered around Poto like a

102

crowd of high school students cheering their homecoming queen.

Leaf arrived on his Bramble Mat and hovered close above the bank. It looked like he had won this part of the race.

"Poto's in the lake, right?" he asked Zohna. She nodded with a playful wink.

He flew his Bramble Mat out over the water staying close to the surface to look for Poto. When he reached the center of the Lake, Poto leapt up and splashed down hard. She would have drenched Leaf entirely, but he had mastered some cool evasive moves while in Ugly Underhall.

"Missed me," he laughed.

Poto smiled and dove back in the water, her beautiful mermaid tail trailing behind her. It was good to see Poto playing in a Lake where only yesterday she had been in such danger.

Leaf settled his Bramble Mat on the shore and closed his eyes to see how far away Nimble and Pockets were. Before he could get a fix on them, they came rustling out of a nearby thicket of trees where they had been hiding.

"We've been here for hours," they teased.

Leaf saw something else when he closed his eyes. It was a vision that was unbidden. *The collapsed door of Ugly Underhall. A lone figure with long legs and short black hair running fast. Her eyes were angry, but there was a twisted smile on her face. Slithering along the ground behind her was a thick net of matted hair.*

"Only Mee," he thought.

"What's that sad look?" Zohna asked.

Leaf decided not to ruin the happy moment since Only Mee was too far away to catch. They would have to do that another time. Instead he turned to Nimble and said, "Okay...but I was SO close. Now to the Rumbleshed."

"On your mark. Get powered. Go!" said Pockets.

Poto peeked out of the water in time to see them take off and waved. Zohna let out a "woo-hoo!" Mercury looked up, neighed long and loudly, and the sound echoed down the hillside.

As Nimble and Pockets took off down the Far-and-Yonder-Road, Leaf stood on his Bramble Mat and gave the command, "We fly." He crouched down. The Bramble Mat rose up, pulled back slightly, then sped away. Leaf leaned forward into the wind, expertly keeping his balance as the Bramble Mat flew.

Zohna and Poto watched the flybercycle and Bramble Mat as they got smaller and smaller until they finally disappeared into the golden morning air.

WE ARE EARTH-GUARDS (Theme Song)
©2010 Kayla Gold

Leaf on Saxophone

CHORUS
We are Earth Guards
Like the mountains, we are strong
And with pure hearts
We right the toxic wrongs

We are Earth Guards
Our dedication makes us wise
And we work hard
Cleaning up the dirty guys

VERSE 1
Nimble:
What we wanna do is save our neighborhood
What we wanna do is save the world
Find the ones who trash it up
And change their grungy ways

Poto:
We wanna make the ground alive again
To grow delicious food
We want rivers that sparkle
And skies bright blue

CHORUS

VERSE 2
Pockets:
You may think that you are powerless
But there's something you should know
Standing with your heart's desire your
Superpowers grow

Zohna:
So, if you wanna join with us
We can stand as one
To make this world the cleanest
Greenest under the sun

SHOUT-OUT
Leaf, Poto, Nimble, Pockets, Zohna...and Mercury

CHORUS

107

Glossary

Abruptly – unexpected and sudden

Aqueduct – a channel designed to transport water

Bramble Mat – Leaf's flying mat made of brambles (twigs, roots and branches)

Caustic – sharp and bitter

Coagulate – to change from a fluild into a solid mass

Curlicue – a fancifully curved or spiral figure

Dibs – exclusive rights, or claims to

Disoriented – confused about where you are

Distillates – a liquid condensed from vapor

Emanated – to send forth; to flow out

Exasperated – angry, irritated, annoyed

Frozen-cistic – someone who is cold and selfish

Gargantuan – gigantic

Graphene – atomic-scale chicken wire made of carbon atoms

Holographic – a 3-D image projected in the air

Igno-micrometer – a very, VERY small measurement

Immense – huge

Intricate – tangled up or involved

Iridescent – when something shines with an array of rainbow-like colors

Maximize – increase to the greatest possible amount or degree

Metamorphose – to change in form or structure; to transform

Nanobot – A robot of microscopic proportions

Nanoscope – A tool used to see very small objects such as nanobots

Ominous – threatening evil

Outcropping – rocks jutting out not covered with soil

Pirouette – whirl around on one foot (or tail)

Plasticene, RDT, MLH, Ethylprion – names for poisonous chemicals that may or may not have already been invented

Poultice – a warm substance spread on cloth. It is used to heal an aching or inflamed part of the body

Prologue – an introduction to a story

Puce – a deep red to dark grayish purple color

Pungent – very, very smelly

Putrid – rotten, foul-smelling

Re-calibrate – to re-check the measurement of a device

Reservoir – a chamber for storing fluid

Retort – to reply in a quick, direct manner – usually with sharpness or wit

Riff – a musical pattern of notes

Shimmy – to shake or vibrate

Shinny – to climb by holding fast with the hands or arms and legs and drawing oneself up

Silhouette – a dark image outlined against a lighter background

Suffuse – to flood through or over something

Synaptic Interrupter Virus – an infection that will disrupt your thought patterns

Tentatively – with uncertainty; not sure

Toxic – poisonous

Treacherous – dangerous

Unbidden – not invited, not asked for

Vapor – fumes separated from a liquid or poisonous chemical

Words made up by Pockets

Bravarageous – when you are brave and courageous

Certain-lutely – what you say when you are absolutely certain

Coldiferous – when the air is dead still and colder than you think you can stand

Conflaburgated – when .0255 milligrams per power point of crystal solidifies with the urgent liquid spectrum of the designated clean-up target

Fabulistic – fabulously great

Superific – super-terrific

Pockets' Inventions

Carthulator – regulates carbon dioxide in the air, purifies water and normalizes global temperatures

Graphene Radar Razer – cuts and slices things that are far away with great precision

Hawk Scream Collector Conduit – collects energy from the scream of a hawk

Metal Muncher – liquid spray that eats away metal

Plasma Graphs – small flexible mats that contain a special gas. The gas turns different colors to create graphs and read-outs.

Yummy-Matter-Maker – creates any kind of food you want in seconds

Nimble's Inventions

Blasto-rod – energy supply that is quiet and clean

Flybercycle – the really cool motorcycle that Nimble built. Runs totally clean and goes 200 mph –so far!!

Quartaine – a new metal invented by Nimble that is light and flexible, but also super strong

Hey, You Guys!

SCHOOLS, camps, activity groups, environmental organizations, science clubs, teachers and parents, we have a deal for you:

QUANTITY DISCOUNTS are available on bulk purchases of this book for educational use, gift purposes, or as premiums for increasing magazine subscriptions or renewals.

WE'D LOVE TO HELP you inspire kids to come up with their own ideas for new ways to solve environmental challenges and make a positive difference in the world.

THE STORY, characters and song can be used as a basis for special presentations, assemblies, games, role-playing and projects. Special books or book excerpts can also be created to fit specific needs.

AND HERE'S WHAT'S REALLY COOL: One percent of all the profits goes into a special fund that will help deserving forward thinkers pay for college.

DOWNLOAD ORDER FORM FROM
Pockets Production and Publishing
www.PocketsProductions.com
Have any questions?
Email us at: earth-guards@earth-guards.com

ALSO VISIT US AT:
www.Earth-Guards.com
for more special deals
and to become a member
of the

Club!

Be sure to check our
website for special offers

www.Earth-Guards.com

Pockets Productions

www.PocketsProductions.com

Look for upcoming new books
and music

Earth-Guards™
Adventure
Team

Series

Battle at Moving Meadows	2011
Trash Island	2011
Leaf: Sight Unseen	2012
Poto: Pearl of the Ocean	2012
Pockets: Becoming Quantum	2012
Zohna & Mercury: Ropes and Wind	2013
Nimble: Birth of an Engineer	2013

...with still more to come!

Joy Evans
Creator & Artistic Director
Born in Novato, California, Joy spent much of her youth riding horses in the foothills near her home. Her superpower is as a forward thinker and creative, conceptual artist. She has worked in a variety of mediums. For 20 years, she worked with fabric and design, refurbishing homes and creating costumes for stage shows. Current mediums include photography, videography and creative computer technologies.

Kayla Gold
Writer
Kayla is a songwriter, vocal coach and performer. She has written for and appeared in many theatrical productions, and coaches young people on musical performance and theater improvisation. Kayla was also a promotional writer for record labels and music video companies. Her favorite superpower is seeing the magical in the mundane and tossing off funny one-liners. This is her first book series.

Catie Vercammen-Grandjean
Artist
A graduate in Fine Arts from UC Santa Cruz, Catie's obvious superpower is in developing stunning character images. She works both traditionally and digitally during her illustration process. She has been awarded multiple scholarships and enjoys the enthusiastic support of college professors and faculty. Catie is currently working on her second BA at Ex'pression College For Digital Arts in Emeryville, California.

115